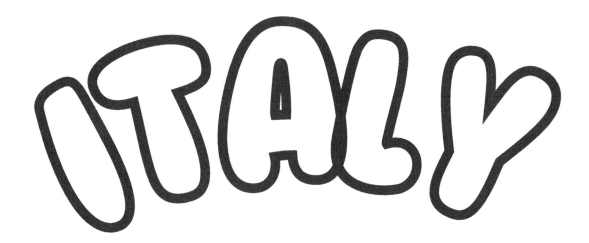

ITALY

Explore this country with colors

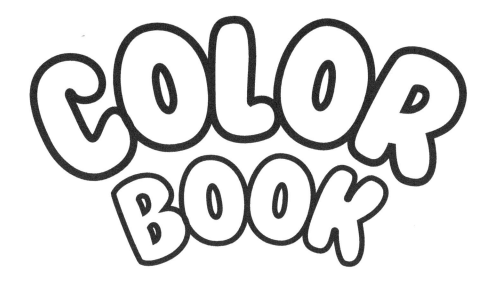

My name is:

....

....

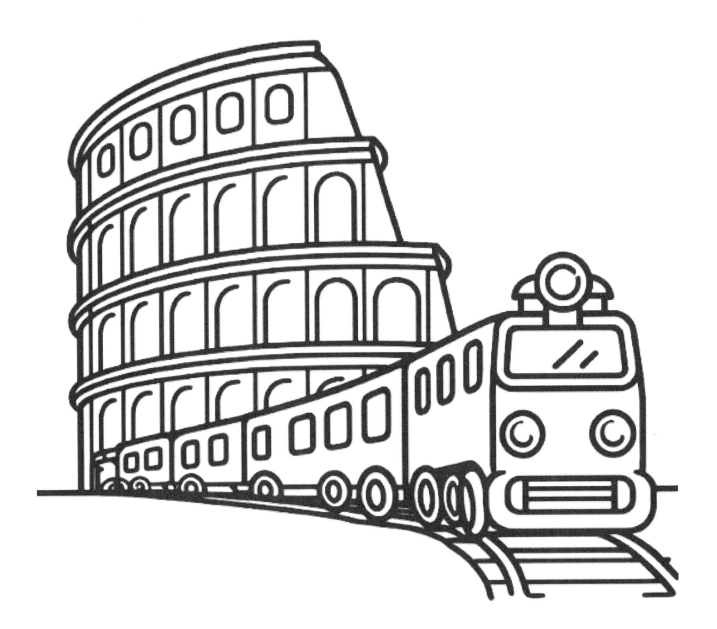

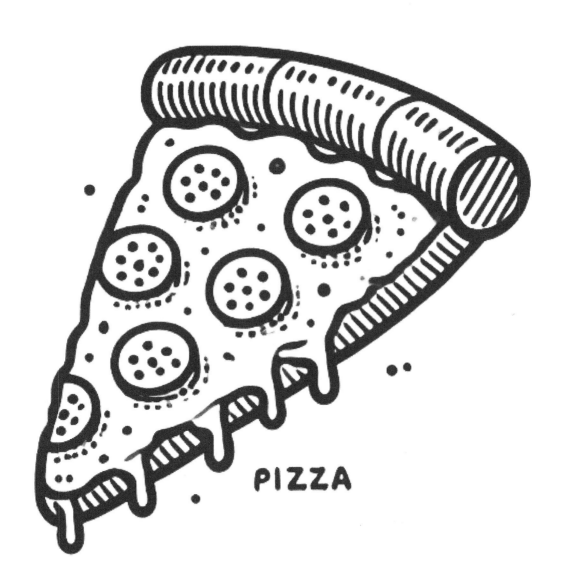

PIZZA

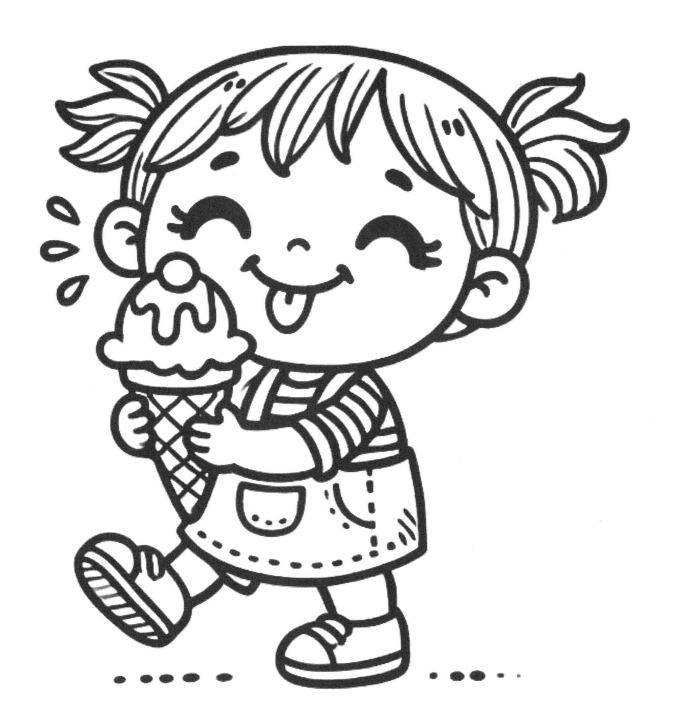

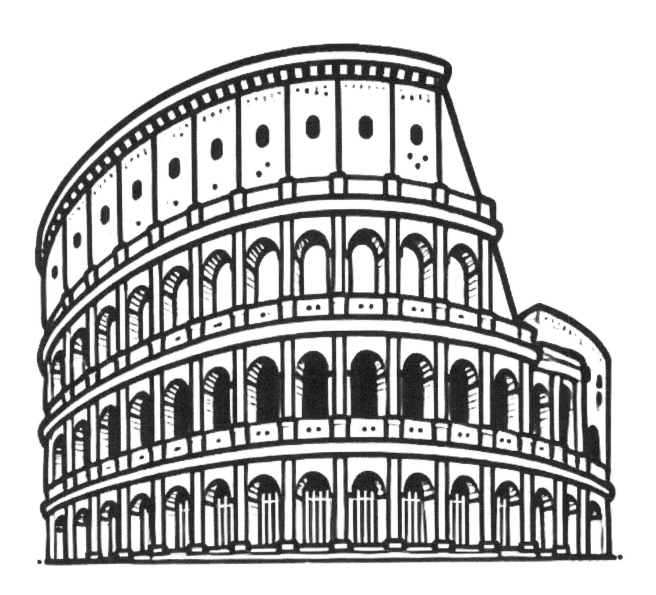

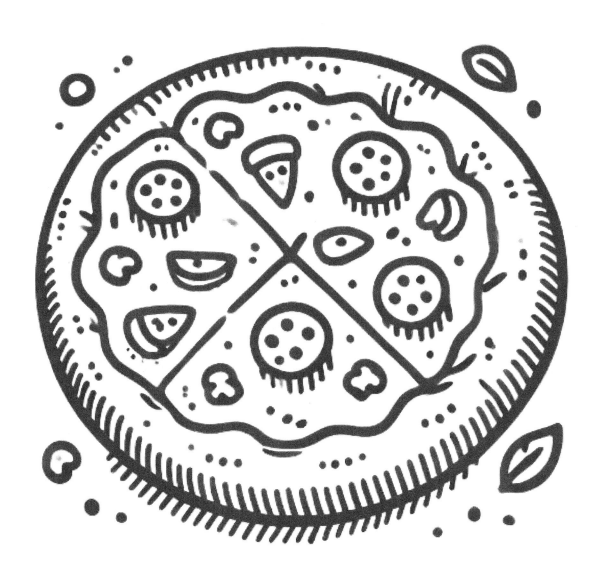

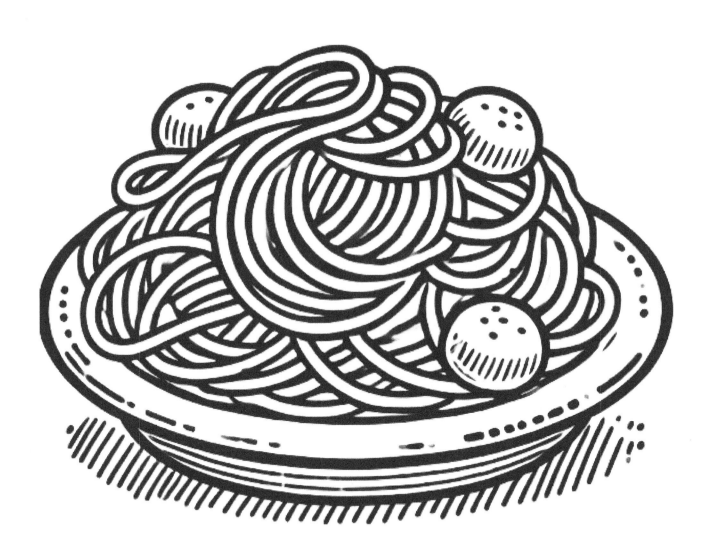

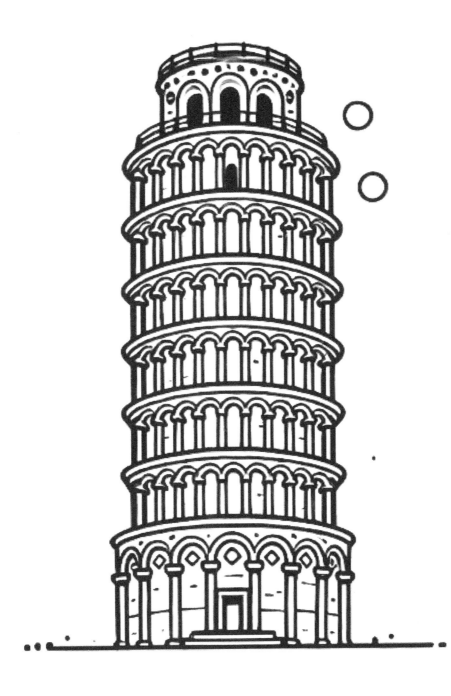

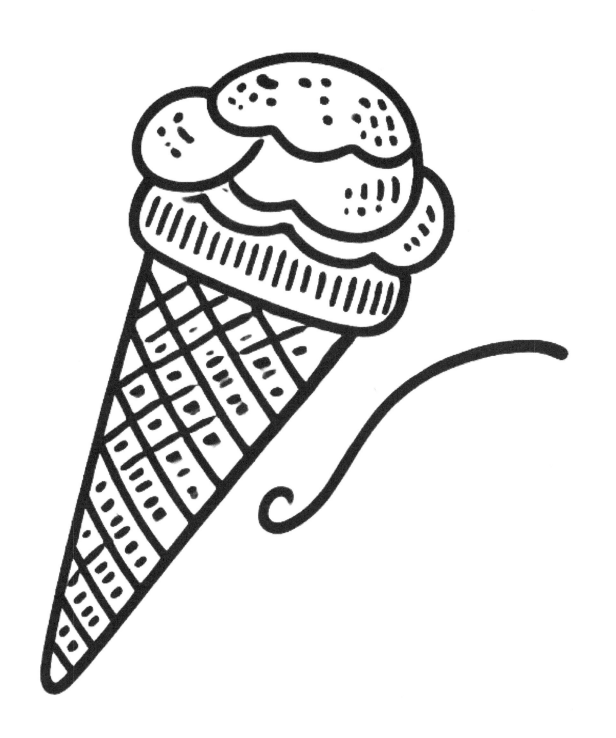

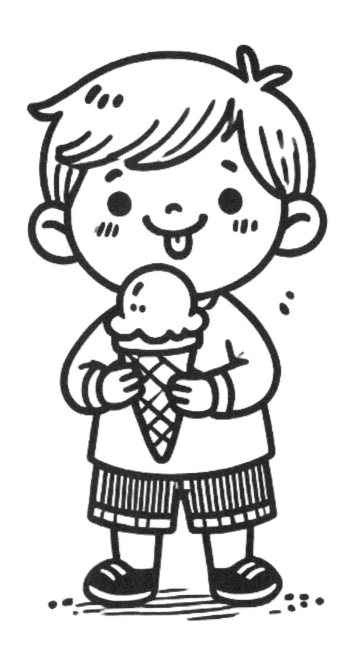

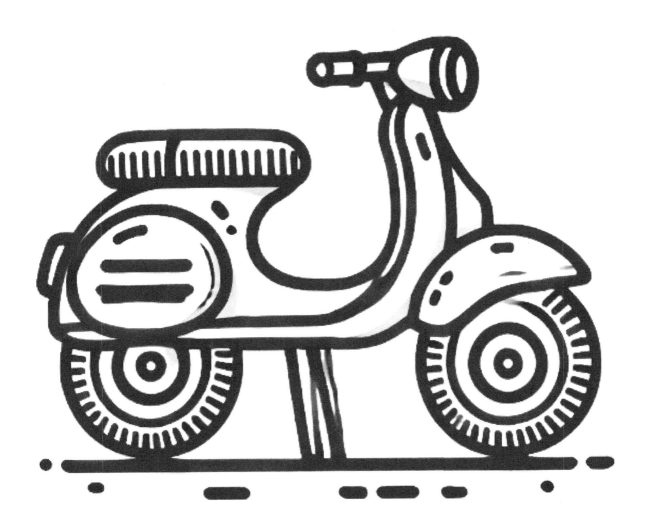

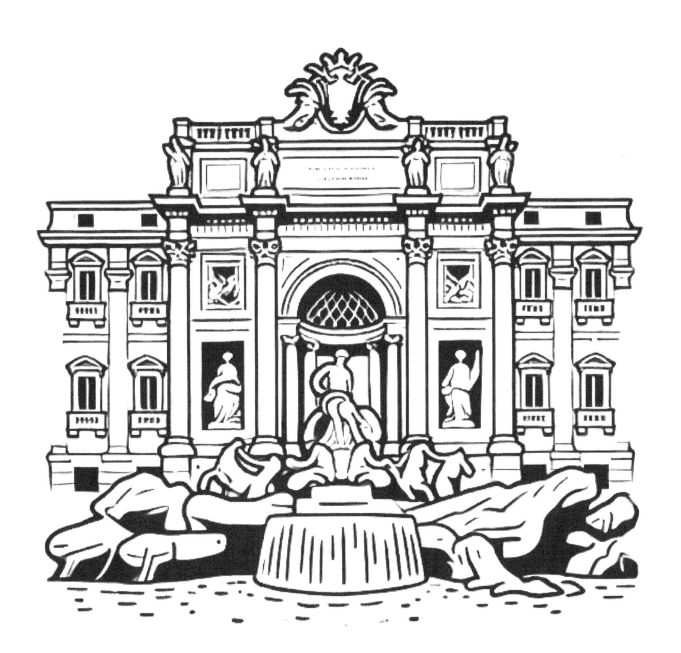

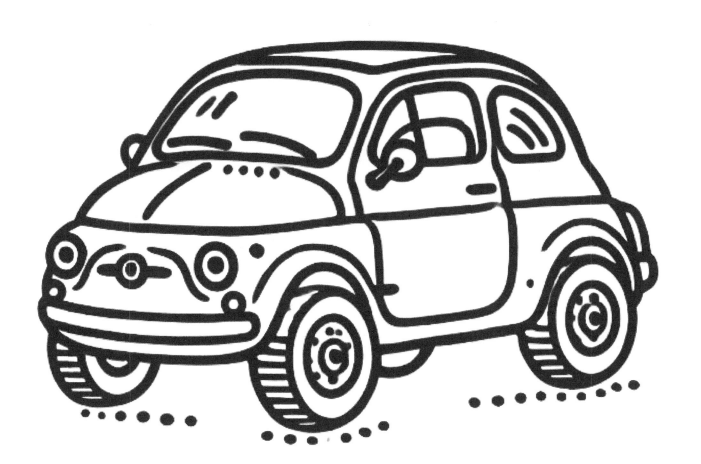

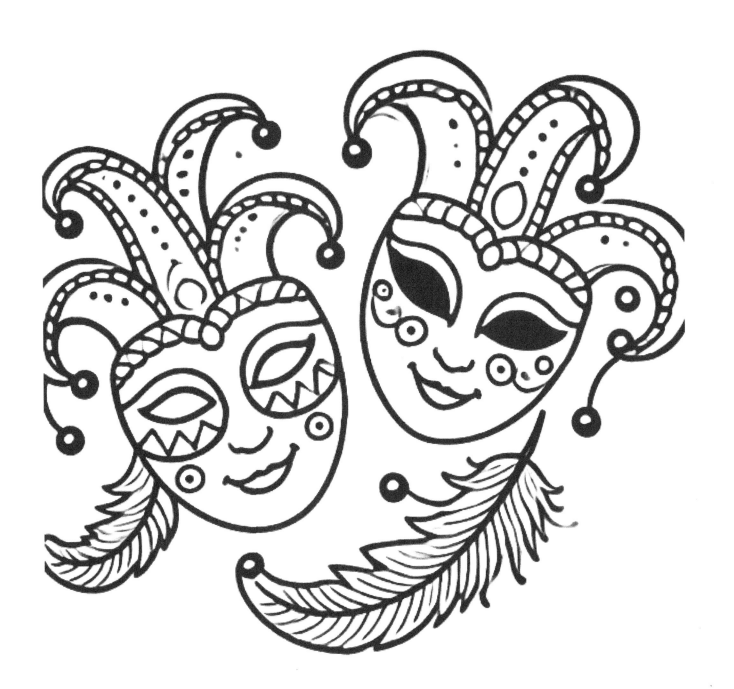

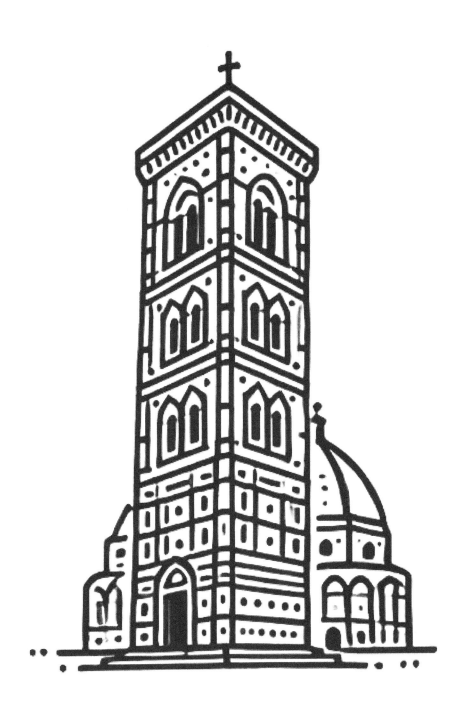

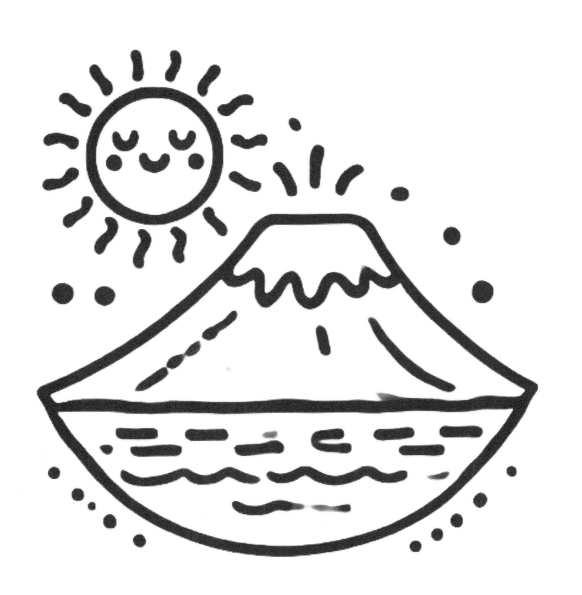

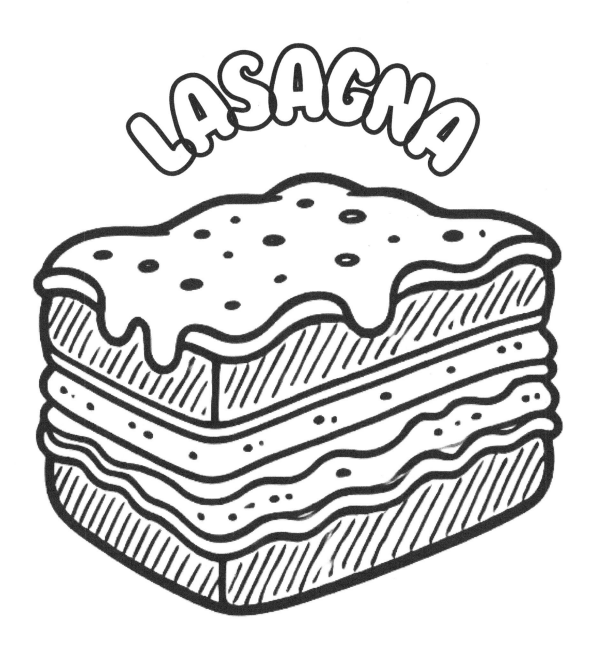

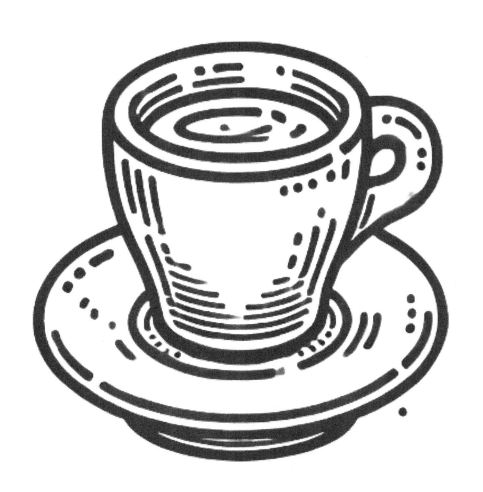

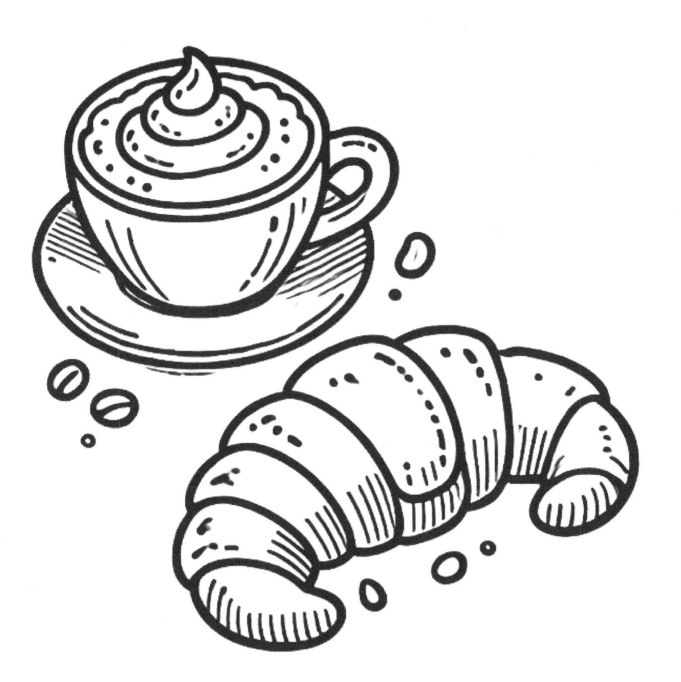

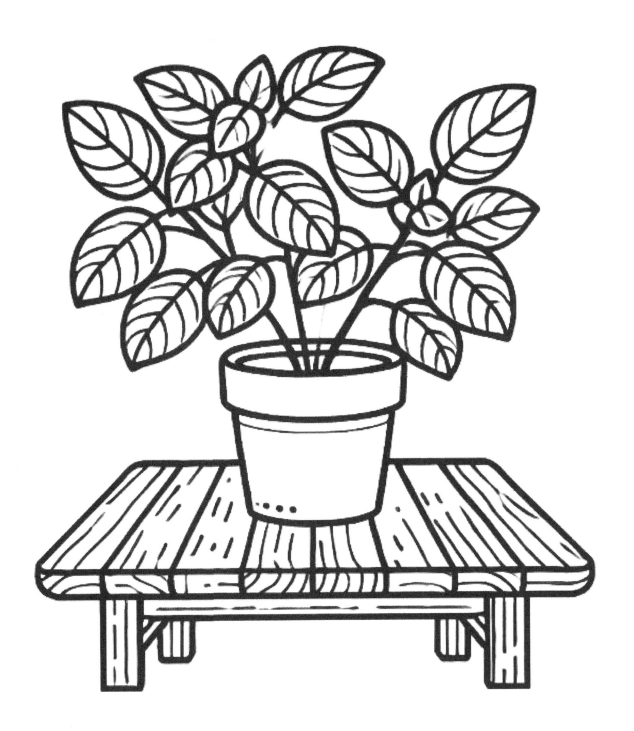

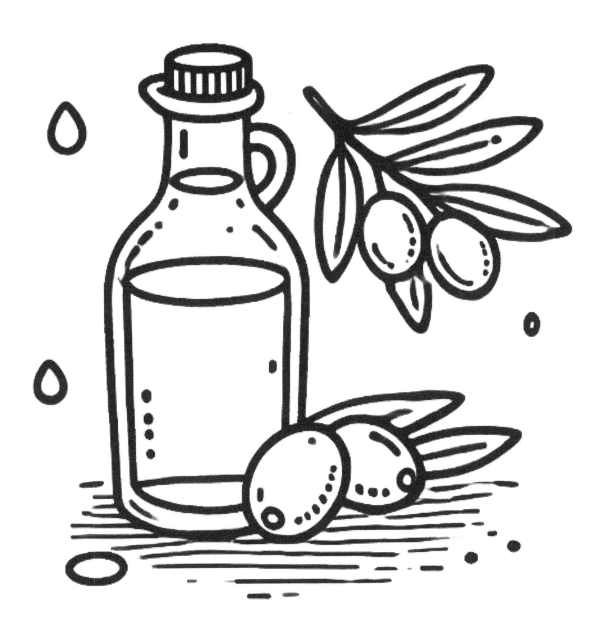

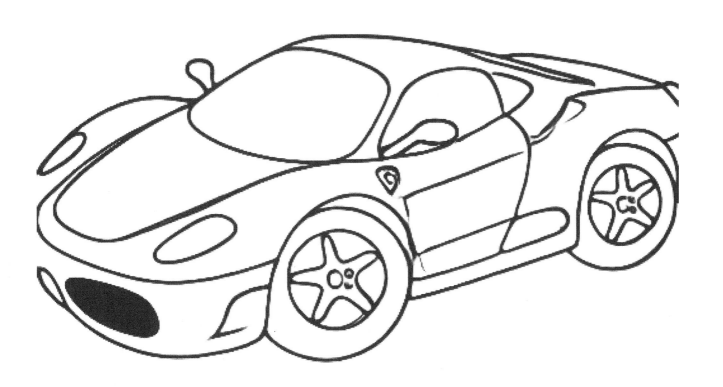

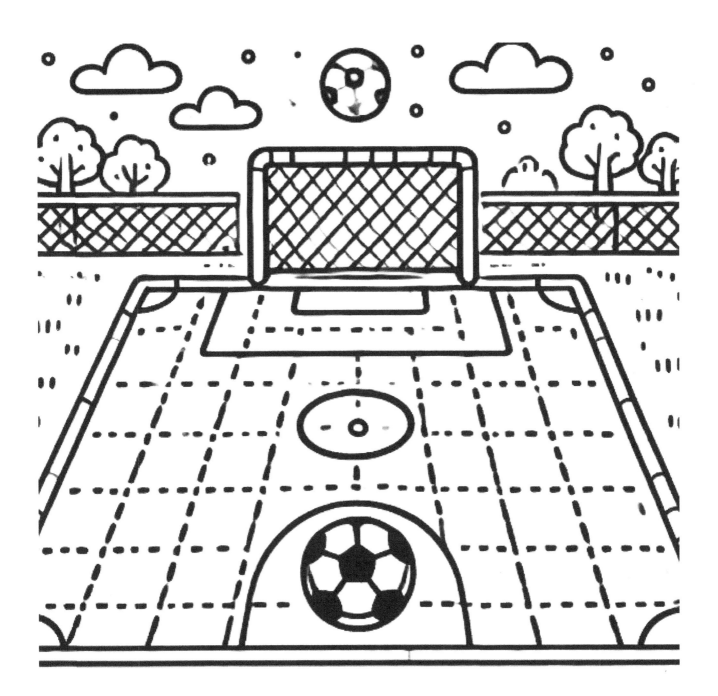

MORE DIFFICULT

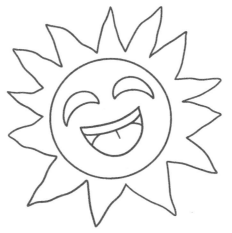

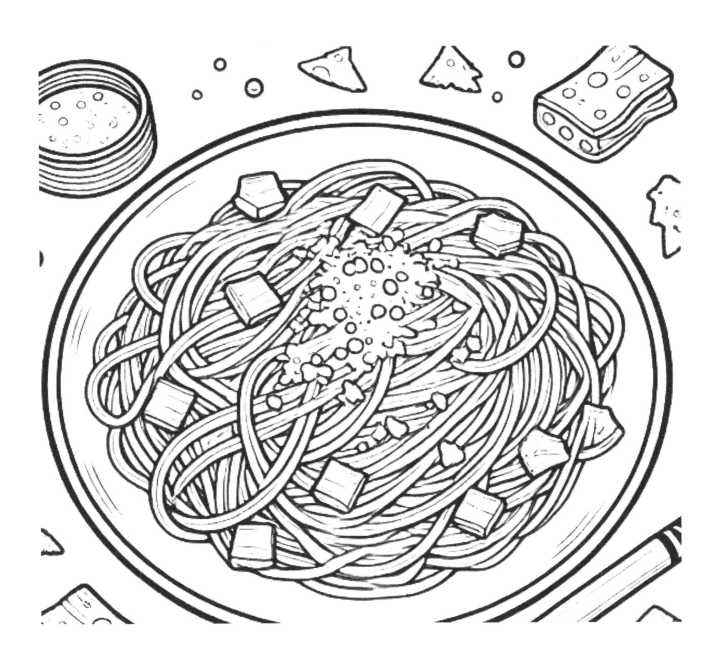

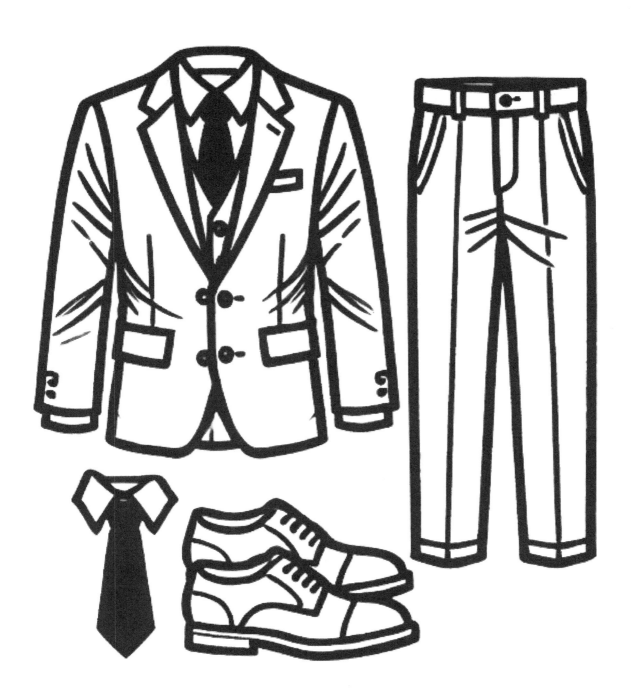

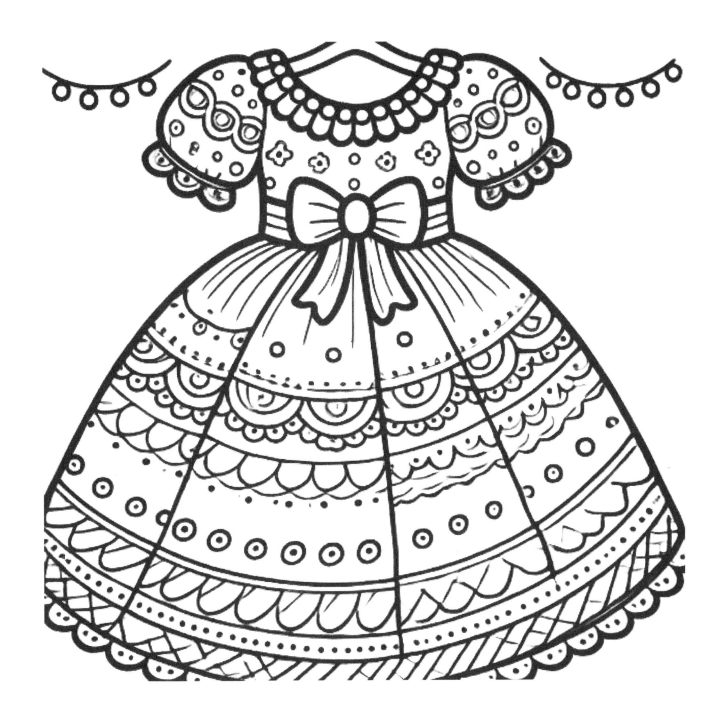

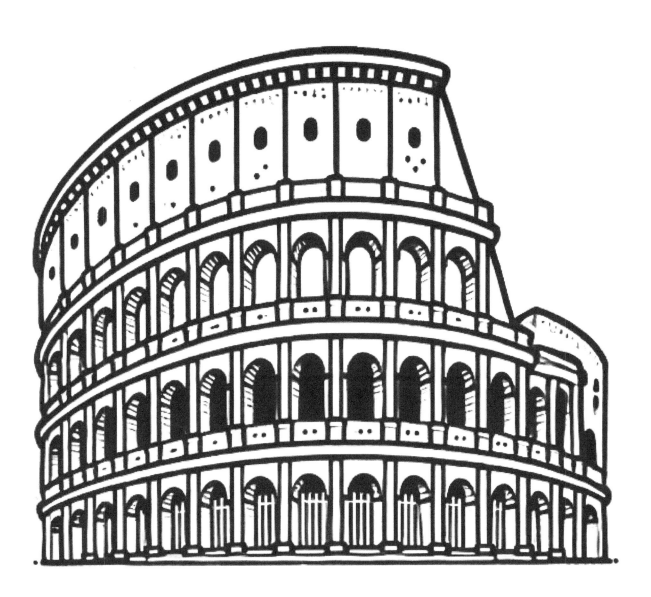

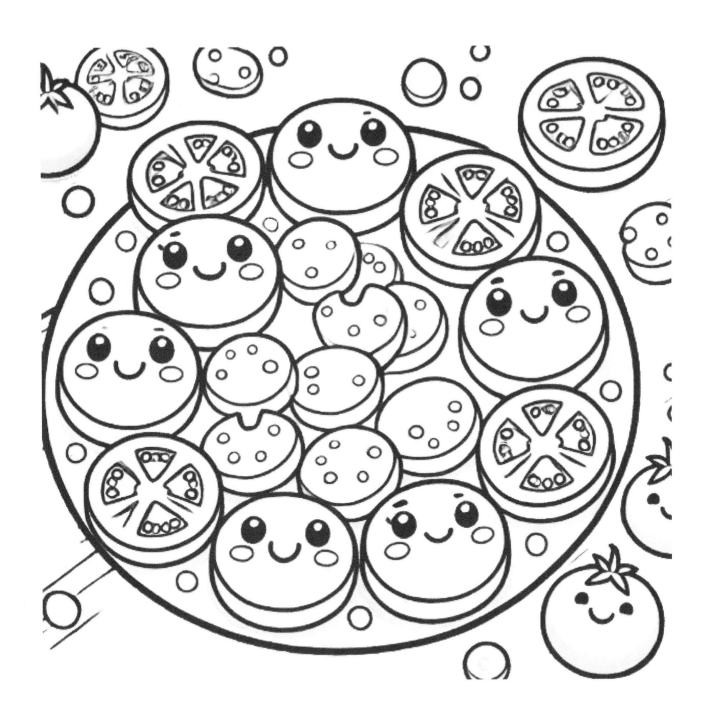

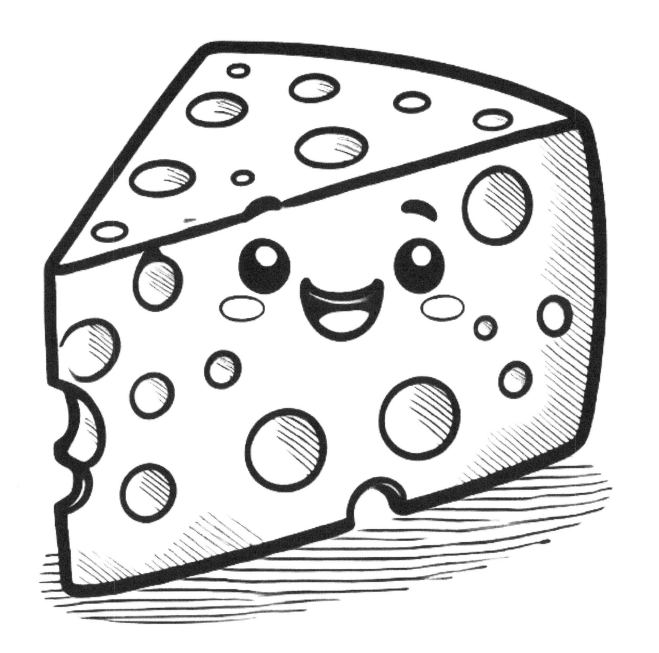

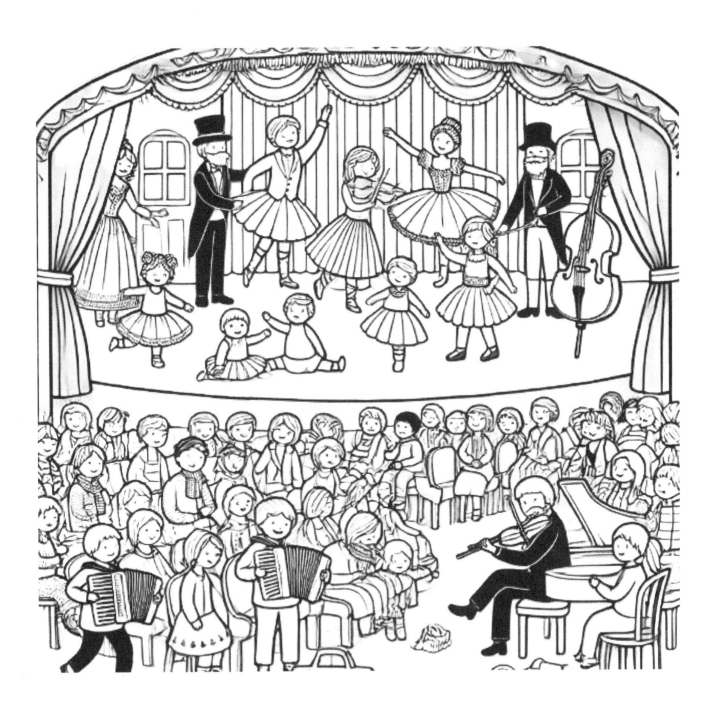

Made in the USA
Las Vegas, NV
16 December 2024

14442995R00037